RAINBOW
STREET
SHELTER

STOLEN!

A Pony Called Pebbles

RAINBOW
STREET
SHELTER

STOLEN!
A Pony Called Pebbles

by **Wendy Orr**

illustrations by **Patricia Castelao**

Henry Holt and Company ❖ New York

Henry Holt and Company, LLC
Publishers since 1866
175 Fifth Avenue
New York, NY 10010
mackids.com

Library of Congress Cataloging-in-Publication Data
Orr, Wendy.
STOLEN! : a pony called Pebbles / Wendy Orr ; illustrated by
Patricia Castelao. — First edition.
pages   cm. — (Rainbow Street Shelter ; 5)
Summary: Finding a horse in the park, Amy takes it to the Rainbow
Street Shelter and secretly hopes the owner never turns up.
[1. Ponies—Fiction. 2. Horses—Fiction. 3. Animal shelters—Fiction.]
I. Castelao, Patricia, illustrator. II. Title.
PZ7.O746St 2012
[Fic]—dc23
2012027360

ISBN 978-0-8050-9503-6 (HC)
1 3 5 7 9 10 8 6 4 2

ISBN 978-0-8050-9504-3 (PB)
1 3 5 7 9 10 8 6 4 2

First Edition—2012 / Book designed by April Ward
Printed in the United States of America by
R. R. Donnelley & Sons Company, Harrisonburg, Virginia

For Biddy and Tala and
the mystery horses in the ravine
—W. O.

For Claudia,
with all my love
—P. C.

1

The stables on the hill were shadowed and quiet in the moonlight. As the two men in dark clothes crept down the long hall, they could smell the warm scent of clean horses and fresh hay.

"Go right to the end," whispered the leader.

They snuck into the last stall, where Pebbles was sleeping. She was short and stocky, silvery white with some darker gray dapples across her rump. Her eyes were soft and brown in her pretty face.

"That's not a racehorse!" the smaller thief snarled. "We're in the wrong stall!"

A tall black stallion sprang to his feet. The men heard his hooves strike the floor. They felt the rush of his powerful body, and now that their eyes were used to the darkness, they saw his shape.

"*That's* Midnight!" exclaimed the boss thief. Before the stallion knew what was happening, a rope had been thrown around his neck and looped over his nose into a halter.

The horse's eyes rolled white with fear and rage. He jerked back and reared, his strong front legs slashing the air. The thief holding the halter was thrown into the corner of the stall. He rolled out of the way just as Midnight's hooves thudded down.

"Forget it!" the smaller man screamed. "I'm not going to get killed just to steal a horse!"

"Be quiet!" said the boss thief. He opened the stall door and pushed the other man out.

The stallion pawed the floor, snorting in alarm.

The thief ignored him. He rubbed the silver mare between her ears and breathed gently into her nostrils.

"What are you doing?" the smaller man demanded. "That's not the one we want!"

"I'm guessing this big guy doesn't go anywhere without his little friend. And when you're worth as much as he is, what you want is what you get."

The boss slipped a rope halter over Pebbles's head.

2

Amy had wanted a horse for as long as she could remember. She liked ponies, but what she really wanted was a horse. She drew horses, painted horses, watched horse shows, and collected horse books, horse ornaments, and horse pictures. She wanted a horse so badly that sometimes she pretended she *was* one. When she ran barefoot on the lawn, she imagined that her feet were hooves striking the ground. She practiced trotting with her knees high and cantering fast and smooth, with her left leg leading.

Other times, she pretended that her bike was a horse, except that she had to do the pedaling.

But mostly she imagined what it would be like to have her own horse. She would brush its big body and comb its long mane. She would look into its eyes and climb on its back, and ride it everywhere.

"Amy," her mom always said, "you know we can't have a horse. Horses are expensive—and where would we keep it?"

Hannah had been Amy's best friend since first grade. They did so many things together that Amy's dad called them the

Amy-Hannah twins, even though they didn't look the same. Amy's hair was braided into swinging black cornrows, while Hannah had a bouncy brown pony-tail that always showed what she was thinking.

What was the same was that they both loved animals. Amy loved horses as much as Hannah loved dogs.

Hannah's parents always used to say there was no way they could have a dog.

But when Hannah became a volunteer at Rainbow Street Animal Shelter and a mother dog arrived with five newborn puppies, Mr. and Mrs. Cooper had said she could keep the one that she loved. So

Hannah took home the brown and white puppy she called Peanut, and her mom adopted the puppies' shaggy white mother.

Sometimes when Amy saw Peanut leap into Hannah's arms and cover her face with licky kisses, she felt a little worm of

jealousy deep in her stomach. But then Peanut would run to her, too, and lick the jealousy worm clean away.

In the horse trailer behind the truck, the tall black stallion and the silver mare stamped nervously.

The two thieves in the truck were even more nervous. They'd planned to drive all night and be miles away by morning. But it had taken so long to load Midnight into the trailer that now it was nearly daylight. Soon people would be arriving at the stables to feed and to exercise the horses. They'd see that the last stall was empty and phone the police.

"We've got to get off this road," the boss thief muttered as he drove along. "There's no way I'm going back to jail!"

But the road from the horse farm ran along the side of a state park, and so far they hadn't seen any roads leading off it.

He sped up. The horses in the trailer whinnied as they were bumped and jolted. Finally, just as the sun came up, the truck slowed at a sign with picnic tables.

"Are you crazy?" the smaller thief shouted. "We can't stop for a picnic. The police will see the trailer and catch us for sure!"

"Not if we don't have any horses with us," said the boss. He turned into the park entrance.

The horses felt the trailer stop. Branches crowded against the blackened windows so that no light came through at all. No one came to get them out or even to rub their noses and talk to them.

The stallion whinnied anxiously, and the white mare nuzzled him. "Don't worry," she seemed to say, "I'm here. We'll be okay together."

She wouldn't have been so sure if she could have seen the two thieves. They were working as fast as they could, hauling wire and fencing tools from the truck deep into the woods.

At the top of a rocky ravine, they stopped. "Perfect!" said the leader, pointing down to the creek. "If they've got water, they'll survive till we come back."

"There's not much for them to eat," said the smaller thief.

The boss thief laughed a nasty sort of

laugh. "The hungrier they are, the easier they'll be to catch."

They began to string the wire through the trees to make a fence.

It was Friday night, and Amy was sleeping over at Hannah's house.

They lay on the living room floor with Peanut between them, looking at the pictures in Hannah's dog book.

"You're the cutest," Hannah told Peanut. The puppy rolled onto his back, waving his paws as if he knew exactly what *cute* meant.

Mrs. Cooper sat down on the couch

with Peanut's shaggy white mother on her lap. "And Molly's the smartest, because she always watches the news with me!"

She flicked on the television. A tall black horse with a shawl of red roses over his shoulders skittered through a cheering crowd.

"Last year's winner of the Kentucky Derby, Master Midnight, was stolen from the Green Hills stables early this morning," said the man on the TV. "The owner, Mrs. Barry, said that the stallion refuses to travel anywhere without his companion pony, Pebbles. The thieves apparently knew this, as Pebbles is also missing."

Amy wished there'd been a picture of the pony, too. Pebbles sounded just right for a round, shaggy Shetland. It would have been fun to see it together with that huge racehorse.

3

The big black horse stamped so hard the trailer floor quivered. Even Pebbles was getting twitchy: It was time for breakfast. Any minute now, someone should come in with special horse pellets. When she finished eating, they'd pet and brush her, check her feet and rub between her ears.

Midnight always snorted and stamped when the groom came into the big stall, but the white horse liked being brushed. She'd push in front of the stallion to make sure she was first. And the longer she stood, nodding her head in rhythm with the long strokes of the brush, the calmer Midnight got. By the time the mare was shining, from her combed-out silvery mane to her round black hooves, the stallion was ready to be groomed, too.

Finally they would both be saddled and bridled. Midnight would begin to quiver again, but his companion would lead him calmly out of the stables. Their riders would climb on their backs, and they would canter together around the white-fenced track.

Sometimes the mare would go around the track two or three times; sometimes she was only halfway around when her rider reined her in. Wherever it was, Pebbles gradually dropped back till she could trot out the next gate. Then she and her rider watched from the railings as her big black friend burst from a canter to a gallop. Faster and faster he'd go, his hooves thundering on the hard ground, his long legs flashing in a blur.

After he finally pulled up, his nostrils flaring red and shoulders lathered with sweat, no matter how much his rider stroked and soothed him, all that Midnight wanted was to see the white mare. Only when she was standing beside him could he relax and enjoy the trainer's praise.

But now they were still in the horse trailer. It was already full daylight, and they hadn't had their breakfast. Midnight tossed his head and tried to rear, but was jerked back hard by the short rope tying him to the bar. The silver mare quivered. She was getting anxious now, too. She neighed impatiently when she heard the men return.

"Get the mare out first," the boss thief said.

The smaller thief untied the end of Pebbles's rope and tugged her backward out of the trailer. She stepped down cautiously and looked around. She'd never been in such dark, dense woods before.

The boss stepped into the empty side of the trailer and untied the stallion's rope.

"Take her ahead—" he called, but before he could finish the sentence, Midnight shot out of the trailer as if he were on springs. The thief bounced behind him on the end of the rope. He yanked the stallion's head hard.

The smaller man was already leading the white horse to the ravine. She nickered anxiously, and Midnight whinnied back as he followed her into the wire corral. But as soon as she was let go, Pebbles trotted off to explore this strange new place.

The big black horse reared, ripping the rope out of the boss thief's hands and galloping to the mare's side.

"That's why we brought her," said the boss. As fast as they could, the two men looped the wire around trees to close the opening in the fence. "We'd have never got him in there without her."

"What if he trips on that rope?"

"You try to get it off if you want—I'm not going in there with him again!"

The stallion trumpeted defiantly, and the two men hurried back to the truck. They unhitched the trailer, shoving it as far as they could under some trees.

"Hurry up!" the boss growled, but the other man broke branches off trees and heaped them up in front of the trailer till it was nearly impossible to see it from the road. Then he jumped into the truck, too.

They sped out of the park and down the road.

Ten minutes later, they saw a police car racing toward them, lights flashing and sirens wailing. It slowed for a moment as it came close, then sped on toward the horse farm.

The two thieves laughed all the way to the highway.

4

Although she had her own puppy now, Hannah still went to the Rainbow Street Animal Shelter every Saturday to help Mona and Juan clean out the runs and play with the dogs that were waiting for new homes. And since Amy was staying over tonight, tomorrow morning they were going there together.

They whispered late into the night. "There aren't any horses at the shelter," Hannah warned her friend.

"I know," Amy said, but when she went to sleep, she dreamed of horses thundering down Rainbow Street, and she was riding the leader.

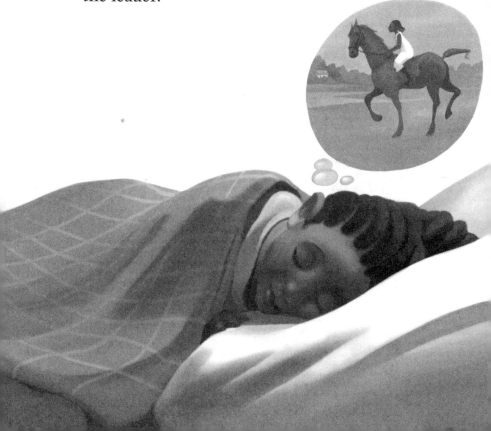

The two thieves were back in the park very early the next morning. While it was still dark, they pulled the branches away from the horse trailer, dragged it out from under the trees, and hitched it to the pickup's tow bar.

The boss thief got a bucket and a scoopful of oats from the back of the truck.

"Let's hope they're hungry," said the smaller man.

"I just hope they're still there!" said the boss.

In the soft predawn light, they followed the trail they'd used the day before and

pushed through the woods to the ravine.
The horses were down at the creek, nosing
for the blades of fresh grass that grew by
the water. They were very hungry.

The thieves slipped through the wire
gate. The boss swished the oats in the
bucket.

"Breakfast!" he called, in the friendliest voice he could manage. "Come and get it!"

Pebbles scrambled quickly up the hill.

Midnight hesitated, but when he saw his friend's head dip into the bucket, he neighed and charged after her.

The smaller man clipped a rope onto Pebbles's halter. The boss pulled the bucket away from her and swished the oats again to call the stallion. The mare struggled to get it back.

The big black horse stopped. His nostrils flared. He didn't like these men, but he knew that if Pebbles wanted what was in there, he did, too. He stretched his neck out as far as he could and snatched a mouthful of oats.

The boss thief grabbed the rope dangling from Midnight's halter as the smaller thief led the white mare toward the horse trailer.

Pebbles was sure that she'd be fed as soon as she got into the trailer. She loaded quickly, and the big horse followed her. The boss tied the stallion's head tight. "Now get the mare out!"

"Hang on—you're not the only one with good ideas." The smaller man closed the trailer door. Grabbing a big pair of shears from the pickup, he clipped off the long silvery hairs of the pony's tail, and strapped the gray tail on top of the stallion's black one. Then he took a spray can, and sprayed the stallion's black back and neck until they were covered with white shaving cream.

"What can you see from the back?" he asked.

The other man checked from behind the trailer, as if he were in a car following it. "Two white horses!"

"And everyone's looking for a black horse and a white pony! So if we get rid of the little one, no one's going to guess that this is Midnight."

The two thieves high-fived triumphantly.

The smaller man backed the white mare out of the trailer, and the other slammed the trailer gate shut before Midnight could move.

The stallion trumpeted angrily.

The mare neighed back and refused to budge, even when the men waved their arms at her and shouted.

Inside the trailer, Midnight thrashed and struggled. He tried to rear and kicked the back door with his strong hind legs, but he was tied tight, and the trailer was solid. He could not escape.

The boss clipped a rope onto the mare's halter. Tugging and yanking, he hauled her back through the trees to the corral and didn't let her go until the other thief had wired it shut again.

"We can pick her up later if that black devil doesn't settle down," he said. "Now let's get out of here!"

With the mare's silver tail floating behind the trailer door, the old pickup truck headed off to the highway.

Peanut was supposed to sleep in his own basket, but as soon as the first rays of sun shone in the window, the puppy would always leap onto Hannah's bed. He'd cover her face with kisses and then snuggle down to sleep beside her till it was time to get up. This morning, since Amy was in the spare bed, he bounced back and forth between the two of them.

Amy thought it was a good way to wake up before going to the animal shelter.

"It's the best way to wake up *every* day," said Hannah, her ponytail bobbing happily in agreement.

Pebbles raced back and forth along the fence at the top of the ravine, neighing desperately.

Her friend hadn't come back. After a while, she gave up and returned to searching for something green to eat. There hadn't been much grass to start with, and she and Midnight had eaten most of it the day before.

Hannah's dad dropped off the girls at the shelter right after breakfast. They needed to be there early this morning, because afterward, Hannah's family was driving up to the hills for a picnic. Amy was going with them.

Rainbow Street was short and narrow. At the end, surrounded by a tall fence, was a big garden with shady trees and green lawns. The building at its front was pale blue, with a bright rainbow arching over the cheery, cherry red door.

Hannah tapped on the door, and they went in. A white cat was sitting on the windowsill, watching them as she washed her paws.

"Can I help you?" squawked a gray parrot on a perch above the desk.

Amy laughed.

"Gulliver thinks he's the receptionist," Hannah explained.

Mona came in from the small animal room, with her little dog, Nelly, following close behind. "Where would you most like to help?" she asked Amy.

"Are there any horses?" Amy asked, just in case her dream had been a little bit true.

Mona shook her head. "You never know what's going to turn up here next, but we haven't had a lost horse for ages."

So Amy took some hay out to Fred, the three-legged goat, and checked that his water trough was full. Juan arrived and showed her how to brush the goat's coat to get all the extra hair out and keep his skin healthy. Fred liked being groomed. He leaned against her as she brushed, and rubbed his head against her back when she finished.

"He's saying thank you," said Juan.

5

Molly and Peanut were in the car when Hannah's parents picked the girls up from Rainbow Street. "They're part of the family," Mr. Cooper said. "We couldn't go on a picnic without them!"

They drove along the coast for nearly half an hour before Hannah's dad turned onto the road into the hills. Hannah and Amy were getting bored in the back seat. Peanut raced back and forth, standing on Hannah's legs to look out the right-hand window, then on Amy's to look out the left. He was cute, but his claws were sharp.

His shaggy white mother sat quietly at Mrs. Cooper's feet. Every few minutes, she'd stroke the dog's ears, and Molly would look up adoringly at her.

Peanut loved Hannah, but he was too busy to stop and look at her.

"Nearly there!" Hannah's dad said, pointing to a sign.

They kept on driving. Now the road wound along between the hills and trees of the park on one side and farms on the other. Amy gazed out at the farms, hoping to see horses. So far all she'd seen were sheep.

The day would be perfect if she could just see a horse.

Pebbles had covered every inch of the wire corral. She'd scrambled down to the creek to drink and nosed the rocks to see if any of them were hiding something to eat. There was no food anywhere.

Now she was going along the fence with her neck stretched out under the bottom wire to reach the last bits of grass on the other side.

She wasn't a big horse and didn't need nearly as much to eat as Midnight.

But she was getting very hungry.

Hannah's dad followed the signs at the

park entrance to a grassy clearing with picnic tables. The woods around them were thick and shady.

"Let's take the dogs for a walk before lunch," said Hannah's mom.

Amy was glad there were definite trails. She'd be afraid to push her way through those trees. All sorts of animals could be waiting behind them . . . bears or cougars or anything. Anything except the only animal she dreamed of finding: She was pretty sure there weren't going to be any horses hidden in these woods.

Peanut bounced on the end of his leash, but Molly walked politely, and Mrs. Cooper let Amy take her. The girls and the dogs ran ahead.

"Stay on the trail!" Hannah's dad shouted.

Up ahead they could see flashes of blue water through the trees. The trail curved toward it and divided at the edge of a lake. The right-hand path led around the lake to where a creek flowed into it. LAKE CIRCUIT WALK: 5 MILES, said the sign.

Amy didn't hesitate. She started up it.

"We can do that after lunch," said Hannah's mom.

Amy looked back longingly at the trail to the creek. She didn't know why she wanted to go that way so badly—she jus' knew she did.

She turned around obediently and f lowed Hannah and her parents on

left-hand path that looped back toward the car.

The picnic was fancy, with cold fried chicken, potato salad, coleslaw, carrot sticks, meat loaf, rolls, strawberries, peaches, and a chocolate cake. It took a long time, and even when they were tidying up the plates and napkins and leftovers, and Amy thought they were finally ready to go on the walk, Hannah's dad poured two more cups of coffee.

"To go!" he said, before Hannah could protest.

They started back down the trail, the

girls with the dogs and Hannah's parents with their coffees. This time, when they reached the lake, they turned right. Peanut and Molly sniffed the air happily, rushing from side to side to find smell-signposts in the bushes and find out what other animals had crossed the path ahead of them.

Hannah's dad stopped at a wooden bench on the curve where the creek met the lake. The trail continued on down beside the creek.

"We'll sit here and finish our coffees," he said. "We'll catch up in a minute."

"Don't go off the trail!" Hannah's mom called.

Hannah and Amy raced ahead,

Hannah's ponytail waving as happily as the dogs' wagging tails.

"The air smells different here," Amy said.

Hannah took a big breath, tasting it. "Wild air!"

They laughed and ran on.

The creek running beside the trail was narrow, but had cut deep into its rocky banks, as if it used to be a bigger, wilder river. The girls crossed the wooden bridge and gazed down into the ravine. It was steeper and deeper than it seemed from the trail. The dogs sniffed anxiously.

"Come on!" Amy coaxed Molly, and they galloped across the bridge, their feet thundering like horses' hooves. When they reached the other side, the dogs raced ahead of them, relieved to be back on solid ground.

If she couldn't ride a horse, Amy decided, the next best thing was pretending to be one, with a dog tugging at the leash like a horse at its reins.

"Hannah!" Mr. Cooper shouted. "Amy!"

The girls looked around; they hadn't realized they'd run so far. They turned and raced back toward the bridge.

Hannah's parents were staring down at the creek.

"I heard something moving around in the bushes farther down the creek—I thought maybe you'd gone down there and gotten lost!" said Hannah's mom.

"I told you they wouldn't go off the trail," said Hannah's dad.

Mrs. Cooper was still staring into the bushes. "I wonder what it was."

"Can we go see?" asked Hannah.

"It's too steep," her mom said quickly.

They walked back across the bridge, the dogs leading the way.

Pebbles could hear voices. Voices meant people . . . and people meant food. People could get her out of this place.

She charged to the top of the bank, whinnying loudly. She whinnied again as she trotted back and forth through the trees along the fence.

No one came.

"Did you hear that?" Amy asked. "It sounded like a horse!"

They were back on the trail around the lake. Everyone stopped and listened. Birds called, and frogs croaked. No one could hear anything else.

"You've got horses on the brain," Hannah teased.

They kept on going.

The thieves had been driving all day. Their old truck was hot and dusty, and they were hot and thirsty.

At lunchtime they pulled into a gas station. "Gas and go!" said the boss thief, and the smaller man jumped out.

Midnight started kicking. He thrashed and reared till the whole trailer rocked and a hoof-sized dent appeared in the gate. People filling their cars stared.

"Is that horse okay?" called a woman in cowboy boots, coming toward them.

The small thief dropped the gas hose before he had time to start it and jumped back into the truck. "The shaving cream's worn off!" he hissed.

The driver swung back onto the highway so fast the tires squealed. The horse trailer rattled behind, with Midnight still kicking and trumpeting.

"We'll take the back road," the boss thief decided. "We don't want anyone else looking at him."

"Not till we sell him!" said the smaller thief, rubbing his hands together greedily.

The back road was twisty and narrow. There were no gas stations. An hour later, the thieves were sweating and the truck was spluttering.

"What if we run out of gas?" the smaller man asked nervously.

"We won't," said the boss, slowing down to turn into a driveway with tall black gates. "That's where we're going!"

The truck coughed, shuddered—and stopped in the middle of the road.

"Get out and push!" shouted the boss.

"I can't push a truck and trailer!" the smaller thief shouted back. "Just get the horse out!"

They were shouting so loudly they didn't hear the police car till it was right behind them.

6

Maybe Hannah's right, Amy thought. *Maybe I do just have horses on the brain.*

Her mom always said that, too. Especially when Amy drew horses all over her homework or when she practiced galloping around the backyard.

But usually, no matter how much she daydreamed or how hard she imagined riding, Amy knew that the horses were imaginary. This was the first time she'd ever thought she'd heard a real one.

The silver mare gave up whinnying and went on searching for food. She noticed a scrubby tree on the other side of the fence. It didn't look like anything she'd ever eaten before, but it was green and fresh. She stuck her head through the two middle wires of the corral and snatched a mouthful of leaves.

Her rope halter caught on a twist of wire. The pony tugged, and the wire slipped farther through the nose strap.

The harder she tugged, the tighter the wire got.

Pebbles was stuck with her head between the two wires of the fence.

The trail took Amy and the Coopers right around the lake. Near the end, the trail forked again, with a shortcut leading straight back to the picnic site. The other path looped back toward the creek and ended up where they'd begun.

"I know which way I'm going," said Hannah's mom, turning onto the shortcut.

"But we wanted to finish the whole trail!" said Hannah.

Her dad laughed. "Okay, you two can

do that last half mile. Take the dogs and stay on the trail. We'll meet you at the other end."

The girls grinned at each other. They both wanted to say that they'd walked five miles. It hadn't been nearly as hard as it sounded.

"It's always better walking with the dogs," said Hannah.

"Especially now that your mom lets me take Molly," said Amy.

Ten minutes later, when the end of the trail was nearly in sight, they heard it again: a horse whinnying. Peanut barked, and Molly stopped to listen.

"That did sound like a horse," Hannah admitted.

"But it seems like it's back at the creek. Nobody would be riding there!"

They turned and ran back toward the sound. Here, the trail ran along the top of the ravine for about a hundred yards. Amy knew for sure they hadn't seen a horse when they'd walked along it a few minutes ago—and there definitely wasn't a horse there now.

"We'll have to go back," said Hannah. "Mom and Dad will be wondering where we are."

Amy nodded and turned around with her friend. There was nothing else she could do. If they really had heard a horse, its rider would look after it. The horse didn't need her.

Then, just as they were nearly back at the end of the trail, Molly dashed into the woods. She yanked so hard she nearly pulled Amy off her feet.

"Whoa!" Amy shouted.

And a horse neighed back. It was the strangest neigh Amy had ever heard, but it definitely came from a horse.

Amy raced into the woods after the little dog.

Hannah hesitated for a moment and followed.

Pebbles was normally calm and quiet, but her head had been stuck through a fence for nearly an hour. The more she struggled, the tighter the rope strap pulled, and the tighter it pulled, the more panicky she got. By the time Amy burst through the woods, the mare's ears were laid back flat with fear, and her silvery shoulders were covered with sweat.

The dogs barked frantically. Amy pulled Molly back.

"It's okay, horse," she said, trying to keep her voice low and comforting. "I'll help you."

"I'll get Dad!" Hannah called. "He can cut the wire!"

"Take the dogs," Amy said. "They're scaring it."

Hannah grabbed both leashes and raced back through the trees.

Amy came closer. None of the horse books she'd read or shows she'd watched had ever told her how to untangle a horse with its halter caught through a wire.

But the horse couldn't wait for Hannah to come back with her mom and dad. Amy had to do something now.

The wire hook was poking through

the side of the noseband. A smear of red blood stained the horse's silvery muzzle, where the wire and rope had rubbed the skin raw.

Amy tried everything she could think of. She tried to pull the rope band off the wire, tried to straighten out the wire, tried to undo the halter's rope knot. Nothing worked. The wire was too strong, and the rope was pulled too tight. Her fingers couldn't even loosen the knot. Amy's eyes filled with tears as the mare pulled back again, yanking the halter tighter on her head.

"NO!" Amy said desperately. "Bring your head forward!"

The terrified horse rolled her eyes.

Amy put her arms around the big white head and tried to pull it forward. The mare was too frightened now to know that she was being helped. She pulled back harder.

"Come on," Amy coaxed. She was still trying to sound calm, but her voice was squeaky and her hands were trembling. Angrily, she brushed her tears away. She was never going to be able to help this horse if she kept crying.

But she knew she wasn't strong enough to pull the terrified horse's head forward and down, the way it needed to go. Not from the ground.

Amy looked toward the trail. There was no sign of Hannah and her parents.

"You've got to trust me, horse!" she

said. "Just like I've got to trust you." She knew that it was dangerous to jump onto a horse she didn't know, with no saddle or bridle or anyone else around. There just wasn't any other way she could save it.

The horse's back was higher than Amy's head, but the ground was steep. Amy stood on a rock and grabbed the silvery mane with both hands.

The first time she tried to jump, she was standing too far away, and she fell off her rock without touching the horse. She tried again, landed against the horse's back, and slipped straight down.

But I've got to do it! she thought. *Nothing else is going to work.*

She grabbed the mane again, jumped,

pulled herself up . . . and landed across the horse's back, with her head on one side and her feet on the other.

At the back of her mind, Amy was surprised that she'd actually done it, but she didn't have time to think. She swung her right leg over the horse's rump and sat up as if she were ready to ride.

She was so scared and excited she could hardly breathe.

The mare didn't seem to notice. She was still yanking at the fence.

"Come on, Silvie," Amy said. She'd thought she was going to say "Silver," but when it came out, Silvie seemed like a better name for such a pretty horse. She squeezed her legs against the round white sides the way riders did in horse books.

Silvie didn't move. Amy squeezed again, harder, and clucked the way a horse whisperer did in a show she'd watched.

The horse swayed, as if she was thinking about moving.

Amy went on squeezing and leaning

forward at the same time, sliding all her weight onto Silvie's head, pushing it down as hard as she could. The horse took one step toward the fence, shifting her head just a few inches farther out and down.

The halter unhooked itself from the wire.

The horse backed quickly away from the fence. Amy slid down the smooth silvery neck and tumbled onto the ground just as Hannah and her parents rushed up to the corral.

7

Hannah's mom was mostly worried about whether Amy was okay.

Hannah's dad was wondering how and why the horse was there.

Hannah couldn't believe that her horse-crazy friend had not only found a horse but had sort of ridden and rescued one.

Amy was full of the warm smell of

horse and so jumbled with emotions that she didn't know what she thought.

She wanted to laugh because Silvie was nuzzling her face, as if she was checking that Amy was okay, and she'd never known that a horse's lips would be so rubbery and tickly. She was glowing with happiness because Silvie liked her. She was just about bursting with excitement that she'd gotten onto a horse all by herself, even if she had fallen off in three seconds. She was sad about the cut on Silvie's face and angry when she noticed that her tail had been chopped off so that she couldn't swish away flies.

But most of all, Amy was worried about what they were going to do with Silvie

first Amy's mother thought it was a joke when Amy said she'd found a horse.

"She really did," Hannah's mom said.

"Rescued it!" said Hannah's dad.

"I'm very proud of you, Amy," her mom said. "And I wish I could say that you could keep it. But even if they can't find out who it belongs to, there's absolutely no way we can have a horse."

"I know," Amy whispered, although deep down inside she'd been wishing exactly that. She gave the phone back to Hannah's mom and went on patting the horse's face. Silvie was busy checking the ground for any blade of grass she might have missed, but she didn't mind Hannah petting her at the same time.

Amy wished she had something for her to eat. "When I was little," she told Hannah, "I always used to put a carrot in my pocket, just in case I met a horse."

Hannah laughed. "I carried crackers in my pockets in case I met a dog."

"So that's why dogs always followed you!" exclaimed her dad.

"I think we've got carrot sticks left from the picnic," said her mom. "The horse can have those."

Amy could hardly bear to leave Silvie, but she knew the mare needed food more than pats.

"I'll go back with you," said Hannah's mom.

They pushed their way through the

trees to the trail. Mrs. Cooper was walking so fast Amy had to skip to keep up. "I don't like leaving the dogs alone in the car," she explained.

"I wonder how long that poor horse has been all alone!" Amy burst out.

Hannah's mom hugged her. "What matters is that you found her. It'll be all right now."

Amy hoped she was right.

Six leftover carrot sticks didn't seem very much to feed a grown-up horse. There was some chocolate cake left, too, but Mrs. Cooper said it was better to wait for Mona than to feed the horse something that might make it sick.

"I'll pick some grass," Amy decided,

because the grass around the picnic site was thick, green, and exactly what horses like. She packed big handfuls into a shopping bag. It was going to take a long time to fill.

"If we had a leash we could bring the horse up here to eat," she said.

"A dog leash wouldn't be strong enough," said Hannah's mom, but she opened the trunk and started rummaging. "Here you go," she said, pulling out a piece of rope. "I knew there was something here. We'll ask Mr. Cooper to help you bring the horse back if he thinks it's safe."

They walked the dogs down to where the trail ended. The path through the woods was easier to see, now that they'd been back and forth a few times. "I'll keep the dogs out of the way up here," said Hannah's mom.

Amy raced through the trees with her bag of carrot sticks and grass and the rope. She was almost afraid that Silvie would have disappeared, but the horse was still there, with Hannah stroking her nose.

"I was petting her for you while you were gone."

"I petted Peanut for you, too," said Amy. And she knew her friend understood how much Amy wanted to be with the horse for every minute that she could still pretend it was hers.

She took a carrot stick from the bag and held it out with her hand flat. Silvie's warm lips brushed against her palm, and the carrot stick disappeared. *I'm feeding a horse!* Amy thought. It was just as exciting the second time, but she gave the next carrot stick to Hannah.

Hannah fed it to the horse and grinned. "Horses are nearly as good as dogs," she teased.

They tried to feed Silvie all the grass Amy had picked, but it kept blowing off their hands. The horse went on nuzzling their fingers, trying to get more; she was still very hungry.

"We can take her up to the picnic spot," Hannah's dad suggested.

He tied the rope to Silvie's halter, and she looked up, waiting to be led.

"I think she'll be happy to get out of here," he said. He pulled out his giant pocket knife, unfolded the little pliers, and cut the wire. Together, they rolled the fence back out of the way.

With Mr. Cooper holding on to the end of the rope, Amy led the horse back up the trail to the picnic spot. Hannah and her mom kept the dogs well out of the way, even though Silvie didn't seem afraid of them now that she wasn't stuck in a fence. For the next hour, she grazed all around the clearing, with Amy on the other end of the rope.

Amy had never been so happy.

8

When Mona saw where Silvie had been hidden, she said it wasn't safe for her to stay there, and she would have to take her back to Rainbow Street. She put up a notice on a tree.

The white horse abandoned here has been taken into the custody of Rainbow Street Animal Shelter. If anyone has any information about this horse, please contact us immediately.

The shelter's phone number was in big, clear numbers underneath.

"Why would someone leave her here?" Amy asked.

"I can't figure it out," Mona said. "Maybe they just didn't have anyplace to keep her—but there's no point hiding her here and not looking after her."

"Maybe she was stolen!" said Hannah.

"It's too bad she's not that stolen racehorse or its pony," said Hannah's dad. "You might have gotten a reward, Amy!"

Amy smiled. She knew exactly what reward she'd have asked for: to go for a ride. A proper ride, not just sitting on the

horse's back for three seconds before sliding down her neck.

Mona had hay in the horse trailer, and
Silvie walked right in. But once she was in
there, she kept looking around behind her,
as if she was waiting for something.

"Are you used to having another horse
with you?" Mona asked her. "Never mind;
you can share the yard with Fred until we
find somewhere better."

"Will he like her?" Amy asked anxiously. Juan had told her that Fred was
always the boss when other goats or sheep
came to stay.

"If they don't look happy when they

meet, we'll separate them," Mona reassured her. "But horses like company, and so does Fred." She locked the trailer's gate.

"Come on, girls!" called Hannah's mom as she loaded the dogs into the car. "The adventure's over for the day."

Amy didn't want the adventure to end. She especially didn't want Silvie to disappear out of her life. Hannah might be able to tell her what happened, but she needed to know herself.

"May I please visit her at Rainbow Street?" she asked.

Mona smiled. "I couldn't very well say no to the person who rescued her! As long as you remember that she can't stay there forever. If she can't go back to her owner, we'll have to find her a new home."

Amy nodded.

Amy nodded again that night, when her mom sat beside her on her bed and said, "I know that Hannah's parents let her have a dog after she worked at Rainbow Street, but a horse really is different. We can't keep a horse in the backyard, and we can't afford to pay someone else to look after it."

"Maybe we could think about getting a dog," said her dad.

Amy fell asleep thinking about the feeling of Peanut lying beside her in the bed at Hannah's house and the fun of running along the trail with Molly on the end of a leash.

But it was horses that galloped through her dreams, just like they always did.

9

Amy woke up fizzing with excitement. First thing this morning, she was going to Rainbow Street to visit Silvie (she said "my horse" to herself, but very quietly, because she knew that would never be true).

"The shelter won't even be open yet," said her mom, as she picked up the newspaper. "There's plenty of time for breakfast."

Amy's parents always read the paper with their breakfast on Sunday mornings. Sometimes they found so many interesting things to read and discuss that they forgot to eat.

Amy sighed and got out her *Horses of the World* book. She'd studied it and studied it until she thought she knew every type of horse there was, but a real horse was different from a picture. She wanted to figure out everything she could about the mysterious horse from the ravine.

She flicked through the book as she ate her cereal. Silvie's face didn't look like an Arabian's, and she was too small to be a Thoroughbred or a draft horse. But Amy was glad she'd given Silvie a girl's name even before Mona had said that she was a mare. She'd just seemed too pretty to be a boy.

"The police have found that stolen horse!" her dad exclaimed.

For once, Amy was happy to listen to a newspaper article.

Master Midnight, the champion race-horse stolen from his stable on Thursday night, was recovered  late on Saturday, when the thieves' truck broke down just as they were about to deliver him to a large racing stable.

Unfortunately, the stallion's companion pony, Pebbles, has not yet been found. His owner reports that Midnight is extremely distressed and will not settle down without her. It is feared that he will be unable to race again until the pony is returned.

"Does it say what the pony looks like?" asked Amy's mom. "It could be the one you found, Amy."

Amy shook her head. "She's bigger than a pony. She's a horse."

"The paper's only interested in how much the racehorse is worth," said Amy's dad. "There's no more about the pony."

"Poor Pebbles!" exclaimed Amy. She imagined the shaggy, round Shetland, lost and lonely, looking for its friend.

It took Amy's parents so long to get ready to leave that Amy thought Silvie might have gone to a new home before they got to Rainbow Street.

But the silver horse and the three-legged goat were grazing side by side in the front yard.

Amy let out a sigh of relief.

Mona stepped out from the red front

door and shook hands with Amy's parents. "Did your daughter tell you she saved that horse's life?"

"We're very proud of her," Amy's dad said.

But Amy wanted to hear about Silvie.

"We haven't found out anything about the mare yet," said Mona. "The vet will give her a full checkup tomorrow morning, but apart from the cut on her face she seems healthy. She's a lovely, calm horse—doesn't seem to be upset by everything that's happened to her."

"So you're sure it's safe for Amy to go and pet her?" asked Amy's mom.

"And groom her?" Amy asked.

"You've always got to be careful with

any animal," said Mona. "But since Amy handled her yesterday without any trouble, it should be okay."

Mona got a rope lead, a carrot, and a horse brush from the storeroom, and they all went out to see the white horse.

Silvie came right away, nickering gently when she saw the carrot. Mona let Amy feed it to her, then slipped a soft halter over the mare's head and tied her to the fence with a rope.

"Horses like to be brushed with long, smooth strokes," Mona said, brushing down Silvie's neck from head to shoulder. "See how I'm brushing the same direction her hair grows?"

Amy nodded, following Mona's brush-strokes with her hand. The horse stood calmly, her ears pricked slightly forward.

"She likes that." Mona smiled, and handed Amy the brush.

Amy brushed the horse's shoulders and sides, gently at first, and then more firmly

when she felt Silvie relaxing and nodding in rhythm with the long strokes of the brush. The smell of horse filled her nose again; she breathed it in deep so she could keep it forever. White hairs floated onto her yellow T-shirt, and a butterfly thought danced inside her head: *I'm brushing a horse!* And another thought, fluttering around it: *One day I'll have my own horse to brush.*

Mona went back inside. Amy's parents got their folding beach chairs out of the car and set them up in the garden. Amy hardly noticed. She and the horse were in their own world, and as long as she went on brushing, nothing could hurt them.

Juan came in the gate, and Fred rushed up to him, butting gently till the old man gave him a piece of lettuce from the bag he was carrying.

"You're a surprise!" he said to Silvie, crossing the lawn to pet her. Amy told him the story.

"Do you know what happened to her tail?" he asked.

"It was like this when I found her," said Amy.

"I think we need to talk to Mona," said Juan. He went inside.

Amy went on brushing, but she had a feeling that she and Silvie weren't in their own little world any longer. She brushed even harder when Juan came back out because she didn't think she wanted to hear what he had to say.

"You've heard about the stolen race-horse, Midnight?" he asked.

"And they stole a pony, too," said Amy. "Has someone found it?"

"I think you have," said Juan.

10

"But this is a horse!" said Amy. "She's big!"

Juan smiled. "You're right. She's a quarter horse. But if she was working on a cattle ranch, she'd be called a cow pony, and if her job is to keep a racehorse company, she's called a companion pony. I think that's exactly what she is."

Amy wondered how Juan could tell so much about the horse just by looking at her. How did he know the difference between a horse that worked on a ranch and one that lived with a racehorse?

"I went to see Midnight race last year," he said, as if he'd guessed her question. "I didn't get a good look at the horse that led him out of the stables, but she was about this size, and she was white."

Mona came out. "I've phoned the police," she said. "They'll contact—"

Her cell phone rang before she could finish.

Everyone was very quiet as she answered it. "That's right," she said, "a white quarter horse. Just under fifteen hands high."

She hung up, grinning. "Pebbles?" she said.

Silvie's ears twitched.

"Your owner will be here in an hour."

The last of the perfect Amy-and-Silvie world crumpled and disappeared.

Part of Amy felt happy—really, truly glad that the horse was going back to a good home with people who cared about her and a horse friend who was missing her.

But part of her wished that she could have had a bit longer to go on grooming and pretending that the horse was Silvie, and that she was hers.

"Can I still brush her?" she asked.

"Of course!" said Mona.

Amy started brushing again, long, hard strokes along the mare's back to the solid curve of the rump. She wasn't ready to say good-bye yet, but she knew she was going to cry if she didn't do something.

The funny thing was that the longer she brushed, the harder it was to feel sad.

"Come and sit down," called her mom. "You need a rest."

"I got you a strawberry milk shake," said her dad.

Amy sat on her mother's lap and drank the milk shake. Strawberry was her favorite, but she hardly tasted it. She suddenly felt so tired she wanted to cry. Her arms

ached, and it felt good when her mom
rubbed her shoulders.

But the hour was nearly gone, and soon
the horse would go, too. She didn't want
to waste any of that precious time. She

watched Pebbles and tried to memorize her from velvety nose to stumpy tail.

Her mane's all tangled! she realized. It was like a pin popping her bubble of pride at knowing about horses. *Maybe I'll never learn to be a horse person,* she thought. *Maybe I'll never have a horse, even when I grow up.*

But I've still got Silvie a little bit longer! said another thought.

She raced back to the horse.

But no matter how hard she tried to brush out the silver mane, the bristles skimmed over the coarse hairs. They were simply too soft to untangle the snarls.

It's not fair! Amy thought. Hot tears spurted in her eyes, and she wiped them away angrily. *I want her to look perfect when the owner comes!*

"Try this," said Juan. He combed Pebbles's forelock and the top of her mane with a metal comb and handed it to Amy.

It worked. Amy was just combing out the last tangles when a pickup truck and horse trailer pulled up in front of the gate. She put her face against Pebbles's shoulder and breathed in deep.

"Good-bye, Silvie," she whispered.

Suddenly she knew that she couldn't bear to see the horse be taken away. She didn't even want to see the owner.

She raced into the little blue house and shut herself in the bathroom.

Amy didn't know how long she'd been in there when someone knocked on the door. Long enough that she was hiccupping more than crying.

"Are you ready to come out?" her mother asked.

Amy opened the door, and her mom hugged her hard. "Mrs. Barry wants to meet you," she said.

"I don't want to," Amy muttered.

Her mom ran some water into the sink. "Wash your face, and you'll feel better," she said.

Amy washed the tears away and dried her face. She still didn't want to go out and see the owner take Pebbles away, but she knew she had to.

Juan and Mona were waiting outside with Amy's dad and a small woman in jeans and cowboy boots.

The woman shook Amy's hand as if she were a grown-up. "Thank you," she said. Her eyes were full of tears. "If you hadn't found Pebbles when you did . . . it's just too horrible to think about!"

Amy didn't want to imagine it either. "I'm glad I found her," she said at last. "She's a nice horse."

"One of the best," Mrs. Barry agreed. "Pebbles has been part of our family for years, long before she became Midnight's companion. She taught my kids to ride when they were little, and she's teaching my nieces and nephews now."

Amy thought of how the mare had let her climb on her back, even when she was trapped and terrified. She couldn't help feeling jealous of the nieces and nephews.

"So, thank you, thank you, thank you from my whole family!" Mrs. Barry said again. She waved good-bye, turned down the path, and climbed into the truck.

Amy waved back, watching Pebbles disappear from her life.

Her parents folded up their chairs.

"Thank you from us, too," Mona said to Amy when the truck and trailer were out of sight. "I know it's sometimes hard to see an animal leave, but you can see why it's also rewarding."

Amy and her parents started back to the car. But before they could get in, the truck and trailer pulled in behind them. Pebbles's owner jumped out.

"Wait!" she shouted. "I was so happy to see Pebbles, I completely forgot about the reward!"

11

"We're very proud of Amy," her dad said, "but she doesn't need a reward for doing the right thing."

"The reward was announced on the news this morning," said Mrs. Barry. "It wouldn't be honest if I didn't give it."

"Hannah's family helped, too, and Mona came to pick her up," said Amy.

"Okay," said Pebbles's owner. "We'll get everybody together and work it out. But you were particularly brave, and I still want to thank you. Is there anything you'd like?"

Amy felt as if she were in a fairy story and had found a magic lamp. She knew exactly what she was going to say. "Could I please have a ride on Pebbles?"

Mrs. Barry smiled. "I'm sure Pebbles would be very happy about that. Come to the stables tomorrow afternoon."

It was Mrs. Barry's teenage daughter who took Amy for a ride around the farm, while the adults sat and talked.

Riding was just as perfect as Amy had dreamed it would be. It was as exciting as riding a bicycle down a hill and as free as running on a beach with a dog, but it was different and better than both of them. It was the best thing she'd ever done in her life.

And now that she was actually doing it, she wanted to do it again and again.

When the ride was finally over, Amy kissed Pebbles's nose good-bye. "Thank you," she whispered. She was sure that the horse understood.

"See you next week!" the older girl said.

"Next week?" asked Amy.

"Next week," echoed her mom, coming up to meet her.

And so, every Sunday afternoon, except when Pebbles was away settling Midnight for an important race, Amy's mom or dad drove her to the horse farm for a riding lesson.

Hannah came a few times, but Peanut wasn't allowed at the stables, so she decided she'd rather go to the beach with him. Her family gave their share of the reward to the Rainbow Street Animal Shelter. "Because if it weren't for them, we'd never have known how good it was to have a dog," said Hannah's mom.

But Amy's reward would never go to Rainbow Street.

At the end of Amy's tenth lesson, Mrs. Barry said she had something to tell her. Her voice was serious, and for a moment, Amy was afraid she was going to say that she couldn't come back anymore.

But Mrs. Barry's eyes were smiling. "Now that I know you're serious about riding and have a feel for horses," she said, "I've got something to show you."

She took Amy to another field where six colts were grazing. Five were tall and rangy, browns and bays, but the smallest, stockiest one was a silvery gray. "This is Pebbles's son," said Mrs. Barry. "He's only two years old now, but you can go on learning on Pebbles. In a few years, when he's properly trained, you'll be ready to ride him."

She put two fingers in her mouth and whistled. All the colts picked up their heads and cantered toward them, but only the silver colt came right up to the railing.

He was even more beautiful up close.

"What's his name?" Amy asked.

"Silver Shadow," said Mrs. Barry. "But you can change it if you want."

Amy stopped staring at the colt and turned to Mrs. Barry. It almost sounded as if . . . but that was impossible.

Mrs. Barry put her hand on Amy's shoulder. "I know you don't have room in your backyard for a horse."

Amy let out her breath. She knew she'd been crazy to even think it.

"So he can go on living here as long as you like," said Mrs. Barry. "He's yours."

The colt nickered softly and leaned toward her.

Amy felt as if she'd swallowed the sun. Her body was filled with such a fierce golden joy that she thought she was going to burst. She wanted to sing, dance, and turn cartwheels all at once.

She slipped through the fence and petted her very own horse.